AF472421

ANOTHER WHITE SHIRT
And Other Plays and Poetry

ANOTHER WHITE SHIRT
And Other Plays and Poetry

Anne Hamilton

Hamilton Dramaturgy Press
Quakertown, PA
2011

ANOTHER WHITE SHIRT and Other Plays and Poetry is a work of fiction. Any resemblance to actual events, locales, or persons, living or dead, is entirely coincidental.

All rights reserved. Except for brief passages quoted in newspaper, magazine, radio or television reviews, no part of this book may be reproduced in any form or by any means, electronic or mechanical, including photocopying or recording, or by an information storage and retrieval system, without permission in writing from the author.

Professionals and amateurs are hereby warned that this material, being fully protected under the Copyright Laws of the United States of America and all other countries of the Berne and Universal Copyright Conventions, is subject to a royalty. All rights, including, but not limited to, professional, amateur, recording, motion picture, recitation, lecturing, public reading, radio and television broadcasting, and the right of translation into foreign languages are expressly reserved. Particular emphasis is placed on the question of readings and all uses of these plays by educational institutions, permission for which must be secured from the author:

Anne Hamilton
Hamilton Dramaturgy Press
P.O. Box 906
Quakertown, PA 18951-0906

© 2011 Anne Hamilton. All rights reserved.
ISBN 978-1-4583-7915-3
Published through www.lulu.com
Author's photo by Dan Z. Johnson

To the Memory of
Curtis Nurnberger, Gerald Schoenfeld,
and Romulus Linney

Table of Contents

Preface

My rush of creativity started in June, 2009 when I set out on a "deliberate journey of the soul." It was the 30th anniversary of my best friend's death. He was a teenage car accident victim. Even after all these years, I still felt emotionally frozen in many ways and I wanted to heal. The new work that has poured out of me is the result of this process. Or maybe the healing process is the result of the new work pouring out of me. This volume includes new work from 2009.

I started thinking about all phases of existence – what it's like to be in the womb; how we cross over from life to death; and what we remember, if anything, from these experiences. I also thought of other women who had lost loved ones, or gone through trauma, and I decided to give them a voice.

My friend Curtis Nurnberger is memorialized as the character Jonathan in ANOTHER WHITE SHIRT. In this chamber play with dance, puppets, video, and original music, I explore how grief moves through the body. The healing of grief is an ineffable experience, and so I placed the story on stage in a multitude of forms and images. I had started the play in 1997 with Stacy's monologue at Jonathan's gravesite, and continued to develop it sporadically through the years. In 2009 I doubled the number of characters to make it an interweaving story of four couples.

My hallmark piece in 2009 was AND THEN I WENT INSIDE, a meditation by a middle-aged woman named Stacy who considers the path her life took after she lost a teenage friend in a car accident. The great American actress Kathleen Chalfant starred in a production at the Cherry Lane Theatre in New York City. During rehearsal, especially, I loved watching every nuance on her face and in her voice as she brought Stacy to life.

She encouraged me to develop the play more, and particularly, to give a deeper revelation of Stacy's inner life. So, I expanded the piece into THE STACY PLAY – A LOVE SONG – VOLUME I, which I am publishing in my volume of new work written in 2010.

In this manner, I followed my muse all year long.

THE DELIVERY is a short play about Cassie, a very determined young woman who is born into an unusual family.

MARIA, THE DAY AFTER imagines what happened the day after the rumble in WEST SIDE STORY.

HEART TALK features a young college professor who seeks to regain some things lost while worshipping at a megachurch, most of all, her dignity.

In THE LAST STONE - OR, THE ADULTERESS SPEAKS FOR HERSELF the woman whom Jesus saved from death gives an account of the day that she was taken from her lover's arms.

MORE THAN LIFE ITSELF is a modern tale of communication and miscommunication centering on the care of a beloved dog.

In RED RIBBON TIE a young attorney recounts her flight from Tower One when the planes hit on September 11, 2001.

Finally, the poem *quartet for change* muses on the lives of two men who have risen up from the American Midwest – Michael Jackson, and Barack Obama. It considers their hope and vision, and applauds the great gifts they have given their daughters.

Anne Hamilton
Quakertown, PA
January, 2011

Acknowledgements

A special thanks to the following for helping me to gather the momentum to share my own writing with others:

James Harrison, Marina Biaggi, and the Bogliasco Foundation for supporting me early in my career; Kathleen Chalfant, for bringing 'Stacy' to life; Nicholas Matterese, Tom Cavanaugh, Martin Frankel, Robert Benjamin, Salvatore Mascaro, and Carolyn Balducci.

Full Length Play

ANOTHER WHITE SHIRT

A Chamber Play with Dance, Puppets, Video and Original Music

Development History

ANOTHER WHITE SHIRT was first read at Julia's Reading Room, in the home of legendary American producer Julia Miles, in New York City on December 8th, 2008. Julia's Reading Room is a program of the League of Professional Theatre Women. Rewrites were presented at a second reading on April 6, 2009. The playwright directed both readings.

December 8, 2008, Julia's Reading Room, NYC

ERICA	Anne Stockton
MARY (later named STACY)	Stacy Davidowitz

April 6, 2009, Julia's Reading Room, NYC

ERICA	Erika Iverson
MARY (later named STACY)	Stacy Davidowitz
SHARON	Rachel Murdy
GHOST ANGEL	Margi Sharp Douglas

Alissa Hunnicut read the role of the PLAYWRIGHT and the stage directions.

ANOTHER WHITE SHIRT appeared in TRANSITIONS, an international juried Virtual Exhibit at Pen and Brush, one of the oldest and most prestigious women's arts collectives in America. The playwright attended the opening in Manhattan on June 3, 2010, and read SHARON'S first three monologues (Scenes 4, 9 and 13). The exhibit appeared online from June 3 through September 3, 2010 and a copy was available for reading at Pen and Brush at 16 East 10th Street in New York City. The exhibit also included the author's full-length play THE STACY PLAY – A LOVE SONG – VOLUME I and her poem, "Gondolier".

SHARON's monologues in scenes 4, 9 and 13 are published as the monologue RED RIBBON TIE in this volume.

The playwright read the monologue RED RIBBON TIE at the Philadelphia Writer's Conference in June, 2011.

Characters

The couples are as follows:
ERICA/BRIAN; STACY/JONATHAN;
SHARON/TED; and GHOST ANGEL/JUSTIN

<u>Live Women</u>

ERICA	34, beautiful, lively, warm, friendly, open.
STACY	16, smart, vibrant, talented, soft, sensitive.
SHARON	27, worked as an attorney in Tower One of the World Trade Center. A World Trade Center Widow and survivor of the attacks.

<u>Dead Woman</u>

GHOST ANGEL	Lovely, kind and intelligent. She has been on the other side for two months.

<u>Woman in Video</u>

PLAYWRIGHT	40, seen on video.

<u>Dead Men/Spirit Dancers</u>

BRIAN	40 – 45, attractive, well-built, successful manager. Wears a white-collared shirt for his office job, unbuttoned at the neck.

JONATHAN	17, big, lovable, funny, daring He wears a Catholic prep school, polyester-blend white shirt that wrinkles more and more as the show progresses.
TED	35, very tall, frat boy personality. Worked as an administrator in the financial services industry at the World Trade Center. He's a September 11th victim. He also wears a white-collared shirt. It is soiled with dust and scorch marks.

Live Man/Dancer

JUSTIN	32, attorney, brilliant. The widower of the Ghost Angel. He wears a white-collared shirt with sleeves rolled up.

Place

Unit Set: The Ghost Angel's Coffin; Paradise; Stacy's Couch in Clifton, NJ; Erica's Home in Bronxville, NY; Sharon's Home in Forest Hills, NY; The Graveyard; A Church; and the Pool where Brian died.

Time

The Present, and in Memories of the Past. Also, September 13, 2001 in Forest Hills.

Notes of Explanation

The central image is a white shirt, worn by each one of the male Spirit Dancers. Each shirt has its own character, and the appearance of each shirt changes throughout the play. Each shirt is a character in itself, and ends up on one of the female characters.

One dozen red roses are props in the storytelling and are passed from story to another by the characters.

Each couple is thematically connected to an element which is expressed appropriately in dance, lighting and sound.

ERICA/BRIAN	Water
STACY/JONATHAN	Air
SHARON/TED	Fire
GHOST ANGEL/JUSTIN	Earth

Characterizations

In the first three couples, the women are humans who are still alive and the men are spirits because they have died.

The women have speaking and dancing roles.

The men are Spirit Men/Dancers and have non-speaking roles. BRIAN, JONATHAN and TED are dead and on the other side. JUSTIN is still alive.

The GHOST ANGEL is a spirit who is dead and speaks from the other side. Her widower JUSTIN doesn't speak.

Performative Aspects

The following ritual and dance movements, and musical phrases will be created in rehearsal. They will function together in waves of iterations, as in a fugue.

There is one sound or musical phrase for each character (8 in all).

There is one sound for each couple (4 in all).

There is one iterative movement for each character (8 in all).

There is one iterative movement for each couple (4 in all).

(Scene 1)

(The lights onstage are half-dimmed. As the video loop starts, the house lights dim and the actors enter from the back of the house. The PLAYWRIGHT's face appears in profile in a video, on a loop projected against a scrim).

PLAYWRIGHT

The healing in this story comes with the human/audience/playwright's acceptance of death. How do I dramatically portray human acceptance of death? If we accept death we accept life. When I accepted death over and over again through near death experiences I accepted life. When I was willing to throw it all away by obliterating myself, I accepted life. Why are these things opposite? What is the polarity and why must we always swing back and forth? Are there people who don't have a problem just going on with life, happily? Or at least with contentment and a forward-flowing motion? Why don't I have that experience? And what am I going to do with the Ghost Angel's Spirit Dancer? The husband she left behind. Is his acceptance of her death really important? Whose story is it anyway? The living ones? Why do we put more value on a human being's experience than on a spirit's? Isn't that racist, well, uhm, being Being-ist? And does my experience of Being come from the inside of me, or is it imposed from without? Why should I be the person whom someone else perceives me to be? That's what psychosis is about - the inside of the human differs from the way he or she is looked at from the outside. ... *(Repeat and fade. The video shows very clearly that it is a cut and splice job.)*

(Simultaneously with the lowering of the house lights and the beginning of the loop:

All eight characters enter from the back of the house. The women approach individual audience members and whisper one of the following phrases. In the auditorium, the multiple voices sound like waves falling upon a shore. The person in front of the actor can hear the line, but others nearby cannot distinguish the words. Each female actor whispers one phrase to someone, then moves on to someone closer to the front of the house and whispers a different phrase. They can go row by row. Each character says each phrase once. The men hand out slips of paper like those in Chinese fortune cookies with the same sayings on them.):

I thought I had time.
She thought she had time.
They thought they had time.
We thought we had time.
Those stupid white shirts.
A half a tuna fish sandwich, with tomato.
That stupid thing growing inside.
They looked like penguins in those shirts and ties.
I traveled on those trains like an idiot.
And. You. Jumped.
I didn't want him to touch me anymore.

It knocked the coffee right out of my mug.
You looked like an upside down balloon.
You were supposed to go to college.
Black and white, red ribbon tie, I found you.
How much disease can you fit into one bag of skin?
There were seventeen white shirts.
Binging and purging, binging and purging.
That's what was agreed upon. For him.
We come and go and come again.
Astroooooo. Right into the atmosphere.
We had it all figured out.
I should have thrown up my fucking past a long
time ago.

(As characters run out of phrases to whisper or give out, they gather on stage. The video loop fades to a quarter of its strength – maybe an eye or a cheek or the corner of the PLAYWRIGHT's mouth remains on the screen, gently glowing.)

(There is a bench with a fitted, tufted satin cushion, such as would be found in the interior of a coffin. There are red roses placed as if on a body. A shaft of sunlight begins upstage right as if coming from behind a cloud and illuminates the roses on the coffin while the dancers gather on stage and dance. The GHOST ANGEL sits on the bench quietly, motionless.)

(The characters take part in a ritualistic motion to a musical phrase that the GHOST ANGEL will hum in her first set of scenes. First the women start the

dance, then the men join in. After the dance, they exit.)

(As they are exiting, the GHOST ANGEL motions. The lights go to her rather jaggedly. She says to the PLAYWRIGHT's face on the loop:)

GHOST ANGEL

Don't let your anxiety get in the way of the story.

(The PLAYWRIGHT's mouth starts to fade, and the image of her face fades to nothing. The GHOST ANGEL exits. The lights on the coffin fade to nothing.)

Scene 2
ERICA on the Hillside

(ERICA enters. She is an attractive, slim woman, 34. She carries the dozen long-stemmed roses. She surveys the scene, walks to the edge of the trail, looks over the edge into the pool. She starts to cry, covers her face, then stifles her tears and shouts)

ERICA

What were you thinking? Taking a walk at midnight in the dark? I'll tell you, Brian. You've done some crazy things, but that was the craziest.I mean, why did you leave the party in the first place? So you decided to take a walk at midnight at this spa resort. In the dark. I know you grew up in the city,

Brian, but you've gotta remember, there just aren't a lot of lights out here. Certainly not in the middle of the night. And did you think of telling anyone where you were going? No, you're too independent for that.

(Beat)

So you stray off the path by a few feet. A few feet. You slip and fall and now you're gone. Did you ever think of me when you took that risk? Leaving your buddies, walking around a place you weren't familiar with in the pitch black night. What were you thinking?

(Pause)

You know they had to pull your body out of the water. Four feet of water. That's all it took to kill you. It would have been different if you hadn't been knocked out by the fall.

(Beat)

My therapist said it would be a good idea to come up here and visit the site, you know, to get an idea of what you were doing.

I wanted you with me. It was just another business trip, but I wanted you to stay home with me. I don't know, maybe I sensed something was going to happen. I thought I had time. *(Starts to cry.)*

If I had known I would never see you again…When they finally found you in the water your face was pretty beaten up. We left the casket open, but it didn't look like you. It wasn't you. It wasn't Brian.

Lights down.

Scene 3

(Spotlight on STACY, stage left, sitting on a couch with a telephone nearby.)

STACY *(Screams toward the sky)*

JONATHAN!! Where are you????? I miss you!! Why did you leave me? Why didn't you stick around?? Couldn't you tell that I loved you? That I wanted to be with you always? I didn't know it, and I couldn't admit it, but I did! Oh, forget it, what's the use? Are you listening? Did you know how I felt? Did you feel the same way? We blew it. We thought we had time. We had everything and you went and got killed at 17. You were supposed to go to college. To come to my senior prom. To come back and see me star on your old high school stage again. You know I shake like a leaf when I audition. Why didn't you stay here for me? I needed you! I need you!!

Lights down.

Scene 4

Spotlight on SHARON.

(It is Thursday, September 13th, 2001 at 8:46 a.m., at her home in Forest Hills, Queens, NY. We see something next to her wrapped in a blanket, but

don't know what it is at first. It turns out to be her baby Renee. She's rocking back and forth.

(She is very sad, to the point of death.)

When the first plane hit it knocked the coffee right out of my mug. I had worked all week on that document and I lost it. My computer just shorted out. I started cursing, then I smelled the fuel - the rush of the explosion and the jet fuel. I couldn't believe it. What was happening?

The heat made my wedding ring burn on my finger. I tried to rip it off but it just wouldn't come. It was like I had a fire of molten glass on my finger. Or gasoline. The fuel. And the Smell. Of – what – of steel being burned, exploded and then I was drinking it. Like some big fire eater, I felt it ignite my lipstick, singe off my taste buds, pass my jaws and settle. In the back of the throat. A searing beak nipping off my tonsils, and down my esophagus, melting every organ in its path, and to the top of my lungs, like a glassblower nipping off a stem. I thought, "My lungs are going to go, they're going to fly around in there, where will they go?" And then my cilia, scorching, steaming into nothing hair by hair, with patterns waving like a bonfire, waving in the breeze, stuck. Struck by fire. It was over, I thought, I can't stand this pain. It must be...over. Others, I saw them sitting there, calling people on their cell phones, joking. They thought they had time.

Lights down.

Scene 5

(In half light, GHOST ANGEL lies down on the "coffin" bench and places the red roses on her chest.)

(Spotlight on GHOST ANGEL.)

(It is one week after her death. She has a wedding ring hanging around her neck. There are letters in her hands. She sits up, places the red roses next to her, then takes them up around the line, "I felt like Miss America." She doesn't have a name, but rather an iteration – a physical shake of the head, and a movement of her hand which she sweeps from her temple to her jaw line. This action is her identity rather than a name.)

He thought he had time. But I didn't want him to touch me anymore. It was like, "Enough, already," let me die."

(Pause. She looks out at the audience.)

My head was hurting. That stupid thing growing inside. Couldn't cut it all out. They found it nine months after the wedding. And then five months later with lots of Demerol.

(Gestures: "Here I am." Pause. Looks around.)

It looks so different from… here.

(Pause.)

I mean, anyway, how many meals can you eat? How many times make love? And how much disease can you fit into one bag of skin? I don't have much desire anymore. Only … release. Looking … at … everything.

(She holds up letters)

For him. I sent the letters to him. He gave them back. Put them in my…new home.

(Gestures to the coffin. Laughs. As she flips through the letters, on the scrim we see shadows of a man and woman kissing. A shadow of a wedding gown. Making love. Warm, sunny places. Books and lecture halls. None of these is distinct. She is seeing things much more fully – in more than three dimensions, even, but we – as audience members – can see things only indistinctly.)

(She looks around, something takes her breath away, and this happens again a few more times as she looks around at other things. The images, the roses, the floor, someone in the audience.)

…For now we see only a reflection as in a mirror…then we shall see face to face…

Lights down.

Scene 6

Puppet/Video Interlude

(This subtitle is projected onto the scrim: "The Soul Separates from the Body")

(The movement, set to music, details the moment of death for BRIAN, JONATHAN, TED and the GHOST ANGEL. The characters in the videos are portrayed by puppets. They are projected onto video screens behind the actors. The characters react to seeing their deaths.)

[Water Element] BRIAN falls off a cliff, hits his head, bounces into a pool of water and drowns.

[Air Element] JONATHAN is riding in a car. There is an impact. He is spun around, flies through the air, and lands on his head with a thud.

[Fire Element] TED is dying of heat. He is gasping for air and clutching at his clothes to get them off. He grabs the hand of a shadow figure (perhaps a piece of black cloth) and jumps out of a window. He sails downward, upside down, and lands on the ground with a crunch.

[Earth Element] GHOST ANGEL is still alive, in a bed. She is very weak and having trouble holding

her head up. She has a headache. Suddenly, she pitches forward and she is dead.

(There is a stylized set of actions here where white shirts shoot up from the bodies. This interlude has movements performed like a musical fugue. The shirts are their souls, and they fly out through the top of the dead characters' heads. They can be tiny white shirts flying upward, appearing in a video and projected onto the scrim. The video shows them exiting the stage through the top of the proscenium and the sides of the stage. They will appear later in the "Heavenly Dance of the White Shirts" which, of course, represents the dance of the souls in heaven.)

Lights fade.

Scene 7

Spotlight on ERICA.

ERICA

You were supposed to be alive. We were supposed to finish the house. And then have kids. I felt so betrayed. I need you! *(Shouts)* I need you!!! Help me! Help me? What am I supposed to do now? I got my MBA and crunched those numbers! I had a smooth life and you fucked it up. Why do you think I waited so long to get married if I didn't feel like you were the person I wanted to spend the rest of my life with? My life!

It was my life you ruined when you took that last step, buddy, and you shouldn't have fucked with it. Did you think about all the pain I would have to go through? Alone again, after only two years of marriage? Two years. We were just at the altar. When Lisa got married I had to leave the church. *(Beat.)* I threw up in the vestibule.

Lights down.

Scene 8

Spotlight on STACY.

STACY

I called your house that day like a thousand times before. It was Monday around 2:30 and your father picked up the phone in your room. I thought, "What is this? Jonathan always picks up his phone." I asked to speak to you and he said, "Jonathan is dead." I said, "Dead?" I couldn't believe it. "What happened?" I asked. "Car accident. I just identified his body. He was thrown from the car and his face was crushed. Half of his head was missing." You were thrown sixty yards from the car on the highway. *(Pause.)* Stupidly, I asked if I could do anything, he said no, and we hung up. I remember your father's voice when he said, "Jonathan is dead." He sounded a hundred years old. He sounded dead himself. He lost his only child.

I will never forget the feeling of sitting on that ugly green reclining chair near the phone, hanging up and saying, “Jonathan is dead.” I didn’t even care that it was my boyfriend driving the car and he was in the hospital. It was a complete and total loss. You were the only one I cared about. I should have known that I really loved *you* by then. Jonathan was the one who really mattered to me. The only boy who ever did then or since.

(Pause)

Your fortune cookie that one day said, “Serious trouble will always bypass you.” Mine said, “You will enjoy good health.” *(Screams)* JONATHAN!!!

Lights down.

Scene 9

Spotlight on SHARON.

SHARON

I ran to find you - down the hall, two doors to the right. They were hot to the touch. People were screaming. I saw my boss in his chair – well, melted. I could barely look at it, there was so much smoke. I ran through the conference room, to your desk. Your chair was thrown back, I fought to get through – another hot door, hot ashes gluing to my face. The fires. The papers...on...

I felt a hot wind and thought, oh, thank God, I can get some fresh air, I'm dying. I rounded the corner and found you. Ted! Ted! Right on the edge – you were on the edge of the window, and all I could see was a shadow, with...arms...and heels. Her arms on you, reaching, and you reaching back. She was crying. And you held her. You. Held. Her...I stopped and stared. No words could come...And you took her hand...I said...what?...? *(Pause... Pause... Pause).* And you jumped.

(Looks off into the distance for a beat in horror.)

Lights down.

Scene 10

Spotlight on GHOST ANGEL.

(Gradually, the image of the PLAYWRIGHT appears on a scrim. It is clearly visible when GHOST ANGEL says, "Why are you sugarcoating this?")

When I first…passed over…I wanted to go back. To stay with him. To comfort my Mom. My Dad was already here. But then I felt the light like – twenty thousand prisms like in the eye of a hummingbird. Moving quickly. Catching more light. And the light – it was – like sex used to be.

I couldn't step back into that body. That prison. It's so much more…steady in the light. I don't know how long I've been here. We don't really have time, just…being. Being-ness.

(She begins to hum a tune that picks up the music from the opening number.) Where did I hear that?

In the beginning I felt like Miss America. *(Laughs)* Miss America, speech, speech! We met at college orientation. We were in a small group together. I wore a blue-black top and tight jeans. He just had on a t-shirt and shorts.

(She looks down, makes up her mind to get to the point and speak the truth. Jerks a finger at the Playwright on the scrim. Like she has to explain it to her.)

Why are you sugarcoating this? He did things he wasn't proud of and I did things I wasn't proud of. We were humans, for God's sake. Nothing was perfect. Nothing's ever perfect when you're dying.

(Pause)

Do you know what it is to put your soul into healing patients and then they die on you? I was a nurse for nine and a half years. How many times did that happen? He dealt with papers. I dealt with families. And deaths and bodies being taken away on stretchers and eyes looking at me with something like…like I was a goddess.

Why me? Why me as a goddess? I couldn't save them. I couldn't save him. Why did he need to be saved anyway? I provided a place. For him. To settle down in. That's why I came. And then when it was accomplished, I left. Maybe not at the easiest time, but at the easiest time for him. For him. That's what we agreed upon. For him.

Lights down.

Scene 11

Spotlight on ERICA.

ERICA

You know, you were missing for eighteen hours. From one o'clock in the morning until four. They finally called me at work to tell me. I said to Susan, "Brian's missing." Those were the saddest words of my life. "He's up at a company conference in the mountains and he didn't sleep in his bed last night." I didn't know why your boss would be calling me at work. "They don't know where he is." I knew right then that you were dead.

I mean, like, things like this just don't happen to me. I grew up in Ohio, for God's sake. The casket was closed.

I never got to say goodbye. The casket was closed.

Lights down

Scene 12

Spotlight on STACY.

STACY

I never saw your face again, never got to hear you laugh. And my useless boyfriend was still in the hospital. He didn't make it to the funeral. We never talked about the guilt. We were over.

I used to stand outside on my front porch and talk to you in the stars at night. I really wish you could hear me now, be near me now, give me some strength. Urge me on. Tell me not to take myself so seriously, help me with my grief. My guilt. Our guilt. I don't know if you took it to the grave, but I sure kept it in my purse. I'll take it to my grave unless you let me know it's okay.

That summer, Roger and I never had sex *(embarrassed).* I thought it might happen the day before he started classes at Penn State. He came over. He was limping from his injury. His hip got crushed in the accident, you know, while you…My parents weren't home. His father dropped him off. He still didn't drive because of his injury…But we didn't. I didn't know what to do and he didn't force me into anything.

His father came. He got in the car. They drove away. *(Pause)* We just let it go. *(Another pause)* Sometimes things like this draw you closer together, but... *(Pause).* We never really broke up.

Lights down.

Scene 13

Spotlight on SHARON.

(Red and white fire truck lights grow softly at "My feet were burning..." and then build. At the end, they are at full strength as if she is running past a fire truck. Then they cut off at her last word "dark" when she blacks out.)

SHARON

And. You. Jumped. Off the window ledge, the broken, twisted metal. I rushed to the edge and cut my feet on the glass – You looked like an upside down balloon, floating headfirst...softly through the ashes, down, down, down into the ground...Your suit billowing rippling out, that...dark shadow pasted to your side. Like a sideshow attraction I couldn't take my eyes off. Down, softly, the round balloon, like Renee's little panda balloons... all black and white and those red ribbons around their necks. Your tie tinier and tinier, like a red ribbon around your neck, and then I couldn't see you anymore.

The fear began to build and I ran to find you. "I'll catch him on the other end!" I'll take the express elevator and go downstairs and catch him before he hits the ground. I just have to – run. I have to run. So I took my shoes off and started running –

slammed the elevator button. No elevator. My feet were burning...Hot and sharp, glass in my toes and still I ran – red exit signs, how many stairs for each floor? Hot. Couldn't touch the walls breathing sharp and knees ache, feet pounding. Like moles feeling their way along a tunnel. Not touching, touching, others, lemmings running off the cliff together, railing stick to railing, countless, flat steps, jumping up to meet me, pounding, no rest until my lungs explode. Again, to run, no time and then some air, some light a fireman pulling me down and pulling away, away through dust and light and fire and off to find the arms, a shadow, black and white, ballooning, red ribbon tie, I found you. Catch you. I'll catch you now. A shadow coming closer, down like light blown up into the sky's horizon, catch you. Catch you and shadow and catch you some shadow and you you you see you catch and then the dark....

(Lights out suddenly as SHARON loses consciousness.)

Scene 14

Spotlight on GHOST ANGEL.

GHOST ANGEL

We decided before we incarnated this time. Light…was there. And love. We love forever, all of us. We hope, deep and long. It all works out in the flash of an eye. In the moment of a synapse firing. We come and go and come again. So what. Is. The problem? What is the serious deal? Skin comes together with bone and brain. *(Pauses and laughs)*… Ha ha. Brain.

So we chose my brain for the end of this…iteration, because it shows the center of the mind is just an organ like any other. It can change shapes and gain content, not always good. It's the astrocytoma that got me out of there. Astroooooo. Right into the atmosphere. And I like it here. I like it.

Lights down.

Scene 15

Spotlight on ERICA.

ERICA

Kristen and Lisa had to come up to the house to tell me what was happening, because I left when your boss called. I traveled on those trains like an idiot. I remember everything. The businessmen rushing through Grand Central Station so intensely. So familiar, and every detail etched into my mind.

When I got home I went into the bedroom because I started to have a migraine and I saw all those white shirts hanging in the closet standing at attention. Waiting for you. What am I supposed to do with them? They don't mean anything without you. You only needed one more for the rest of your life.

You have seventeen white shirts. I counted them. They are the saddest things. When I was waiting for the call I couldn't think of anything. Anything except that the one I loved was gone. And there were all these white shirts in the closet mocking me. "He wore me. I was close to him," they said, then grew silent when they noticed that you weren't there and you probably weren't coming home.

It wasn't you. I told myself this was not happening to me, it was happening to someone else, it was like a movie.

I had to know the details. I had to see for myself. I'm sorry. I'm sorry this had to happen to you. I wish it was someone else. You didn't deserve it. We didn't deserve it.

I called your mother. She didn't want to know the details, just started screaming. Your father passed out. She had to call an ambulance. I don't ever want to have another day like that one. The worst part was the waiting to hear. But I knew. I knew you were dead. I just knew.

When the call came from the State Police asking me to stay home because they were sending a car over, I was in shock. Of course, I knew why they were coming. Did they think I was stupid? That I'd try to hurt myself? I didn't even think of it. I'm just not that way.

Why did it have to be a police officer that told me they had found your body? It was gross. Eighteen hours of being in the water and that big, ugly bruise on your eyebrow like someone had punched you in the face. They had to stitch it up.

Those stupid white shirts. I don't want to give them away. But I have to clear things up. You understand. It's just too hard. Lisa came and we did some things. But I still feel like maybe I can find a little bit of you in those shirts. A hair. The smell of cologne. A little leftover dirt. They're too white. Too clean. Too antiseptic, like that room they put you in before your autopsy.

Antiseptic. That was my life before what happened to you. I'll never get clean again.

The worst part was when they handed me your clothes in a plastic bag. They were still damp. They were your clothes, but there was no you in them. Your whole self rolled up into a smelly, disgusting, bloody heap of clothes in a plastic bag. All that was left of you. They didn't mean anything without you in them, those clothes. But somehow I can't throw them away. I know no-one else will ever use them, especially in the shape they're in. But I can't throw them away. They remind me of you. They were close to you, last. I hid them in the attic, like a deep, dark secret.

Lights fade.

Scene 16

(Lights up on STACY at JONATHAN's gravesite, very weak and thin, wrapped in a blanket. She has a paper bag with deli food and is eating a plastic container of soup near his headstone. A harsh wind is blowing. She sounds hoarse because she has been talking to him out loud for a while.)

STACY

Ugh, why did they give me those fucking horse pill antibiotics? I had a 102-degree temperature for four days! Then they give me these fucking horse pills and I threw up. I am not that big!

(Beat)

You know, that's the first time I had ever thrown up. Never as a baby. Not even in high school – all my friends were drinking and getting drunk and throwing up and eating too much and throwing up. Binging and purging, binging and purging. I never knew what it was like…to throw up…Not even when you died.

I couldn't eat for days. I think I lost 10 pounds in a week. My mother was worried sick about me. Then I remember. I ate something – a half a tuna fish sandwich, without the crusts, with tomato. That's when my problems with food started. I started starving myself. Then I started stuffing myself.

I just kept stuffing food down my throat to make the pain go away. Stuffing and pressing and pushing and tightening. Until then I played it safe – *I* controlled my future and my present, my grades, my feelings. *I* controlled my skin and my organs. I didn't eat too much, I didn't drink too much. I avoided every type of excess or pleasure. I took in information. I learned everything like a god-damned encyclopedia. And look at me – I want to kill myself. I should have thrown up my fucking past a long time ago.

(Pause)

Look at me. I can't even look in the mirror. I have nervous breakdown every month or on Sundays when I slow down enough to notice how I'm feeling. I can't be in a relationship. I wish I could throw up again. I'd throw up my life and start again.

(Pause. The wind starts blowing harder. She reaches out and touches the headstone.)

I need you to forgive me. I need…to forgive my-self. To let you go.

(The wind picks up to a full gale. She lays her head down on the grass on his grave. Lights fade.)

Lights down.

Scene 17

Spotlight on SHARON and TED.

(Sharon and Ted's dance)

Part 1 – The Christening

(It is the christening of their baby Renee. They're all dressed up. He wears a white shirt and red tie. The baby's in a beautiful christening gown and cap. The wrong balloons are delivered. Sharon screams in frustration, heedless of the baby she's carrying. She has to have the right balloons. He has to go get balloons right now. It's almost time to go to the church, but he has to go now.)

(He doesn't want to go. She screams at him, and they have a huge blowout fight. She puts the baby down and it sits there ignored. He finally slams out of the door.)

Part 2 - Ignored

(Sharon goes around touching things in the house compulsively. Everything must be in the right order. She ignores the baby. She then remembers the baby and picks her up and straightens her outfit. It must be clear that she's more interested in the clothing and how it will appear than the comfort or the happiness of the baby inside the costume.)

Part 3 – The Other Woman

(He calls someone on his cell phone. He is upset and letting out his frustration. Then it's clear he's in an

intimate emotional relationship with the person on the other end. He starts to flirt. It turns into phone sex. He takes his time with the phone sex. Then he hangs up the cell phone, satisfied.)

Part 4 – The Act

(He comes back in with balloons. They are panda bear Mylar balloons with a red tie around the bear's neck. She goes ballistic. He doesn't know what he did wrong. She screams at him for getting the wrong balloons. This goes on even further. She hears the doorbell ring and instantly calms down and acts like everything is fine. She adjusts the baby on her shoulder. Calm and radiant, she invites her guests in like nothing happened. He stands on the sidelines and seethes.)

Lights down.

Scene 18

Spotlight on GHOST ANGEL and JUSTIN.

(The words, "I know you were there" are projected onto the scrim.)

(JUSTIN is behind the scrim, asleep on the bench which was used as GHOST ANGEL'S coffin. He is tossing and turning, within one week after her death. He is dreaming vivid dreams. GHOST ANGEL appears, goes to him, and tries to console

him. He rises, they speak. She consoles him. He cries in his sleep. She is brave while he is helpless. He tries to get her to stay. They pause and feel each other's presence in the way that only people who really know each other can feel the presence of the other. The moment is brief. She must leave. He returns to the bed. He is crying in his sleep. She exits. Lights down on JUSTIN.)

Lights down.

Scene 19

Spotlight on ERICA AND BRIAN.

Part 1 – Courtship

(To be choreographed: ERICA dances a lonely dance. She is in and out of relationships. BRIAN marches in, wearing a large white businessman's shirt, open. He falls in love with her. They slow dance. Before he leaves, he kisses her on the mouth. She is surprised and a little offended.)

(We see their courtship progress in their dance. Love transforms them. Their courtship is about removing the barriers which prevent them from connecting with others through love. He "unwraps" first, enabling her to "unwrap".)

Part 2 – Nuptials

(It is their wedding day. She prepares him for the day by straightening and buttoning his white shirt. She caresses it, and gives it good wishes. They marry.)

Part 3 – Cohabitation

(They build their house together and move in together. However, they can't seem to agree on anything. They try to arrange the furniture. If she likes it, he doesn't. And vice versa. They try to buy some new furniture. Same thing. If she likes it, he doesn't. She is always annoyed. They tramp all over New York City shopping, unhappy and dejected. They go to Macy's and ABC Home, and they finally come home with a lamp. When they get it home, they can't decide where to place it. A tug of war ensues with the lamp. They separate and retire to different corners. She gets on the phone to her family to complain about him. He starts looking for a way out.)

Lights down.

Scene 20

Spotlight on STACY AND JONATHAN.

Part 1- Star

(STACY is very serious. She is repetitious, active

and bored. She meets JONATHAN. She is wary at first. He makes her laugh, begrudgingly at first, then freely.)

Part 2 –First Love

(They are alone. She is drawn to him. She wants to kiss him but she doesn't. He doesn't notice her attraction. He does pushups and calisthenics to amuse her. She laughs and loses herself in his antics. He just loves her like any other friend. He gets up and shows her his new QUEEN LP with all the naked people on the cover. She's scandalized. She looks at him sideways, while he seems to be oblivious of her feelings.)

Lights down.

Scene 21

Spotlight on SHARON.

Part 1 – Jagged Love

(SHARON throws herself into caring for her daughter. She is over attentive to the point of being manic. She never lets the baby sleep or rest. She is always talking to her. When the baby falls asleep in her arms, she looks around. Then she jiggles the baby to wake her up and then comforts her when she cries. She gets up with the baby, looks out the window and then goes to the door and locks it – five

locks. Only then will she feel safe. Then she sits down on the couch and stares at the television.)

Part 2 – Light

(The words, "I felt…alive again." Are projected onto the scrim.)

(She puts a veil over her head and goes to church. She holds the baby and greets people and crosses herself. It seems that she's quite well-known by the number of people who greet her, and she takes in their expressions of condolence. Too many hugs. Everyone wants to hug her, even strangers and it is very, very awkward to balance the baby and also give the people what they want. Someone gives her a dozen red roses. She has no place to put them and throws them on the church pew next to her to get some space. Her face wears and expression that seems to ask, "Why is everyone acting like I'm a hero?" Their outpouring of sympathy exhausts her. She finally sits. The baby is fidgety, but quiets down after a while. SHARON listens to the priest. We hear hymns and she begins to soften. She becomes enraptured. She is riveted to her seat. She relaxes into some kind of transformative experience. It is just what she needed.)

Lights down.

Scene 22

Lights up on JUSTIN and GHOST ANGEL.

(JUSTIN stands behind the scrim. His words are projected onto the scrim and she says hers out loud. Both he and the audience hear her words.)

(JUSTIN enters the GHOST ANGEL's gravesite. He wears his white shirt. It is open at the collar because it is early August. He brings a dozen red roses to the grave and lays them at her feet, or in her lap. Some evocative movement.)

He	I didn't want you to leave me.
She	*(Shakes her head.)*
He	We waited half our adult lives to be together - to get married.
She	*(Just looks – very accepting, well, like an angel.)*
He	Aren't you going to say anything? I need you to talk to me.
She	*(Silence with a smile.)*
He	OK. I passed the bar today.
She	I know. I'm proud. I knew you would.
He	All I could think of was you.
She	I was there. But you did this by yourself.
He	I wanted you to be there when I opened the envelope.
She	*(Silence.)*
He	Your mother was happy.
She	I'm glad.
He	I called my parents.

She	You did good.
He/She	*(Pause.)*
He	I think I'm going to go have a drink. I'll have one for you. I love you.
She	Thank you, baby. I love you, too.

Lights down.

Scene 23

Lights up on ERICA.

(Lights up on ERICA as she visits the spot on the wooded hillside where BRIAN fell to his death. She enters carrying a dozen long-stemmed red roses. The setting sun reflects off the pool of water and onto her face and body. Throughout the scene the daylight fades until she is left almost in darkness. In the middle of the scene, we begin to see a projection of falling roses. They fall one at a time beginning when she says, "Oh, I brought these for you", and then they fall in twos and threes until the end of the scene. When ERICA exits, we're left looking only at layers and layers of roses cascading down on videos down the scrims. It is a waterfall of roses.)

ERICA

I'm not coming back here. This is just one visit I had to make. Like your last night of life. One last visit on this earth. An overnight business trip.

All your co-workers left work early to come to the

wake. They all looked like penguins in their suits and ties. So out of place in a funeral home. Some of them were making business deals. I wanted to kick them out. Diane heard them say *(in a mocking tone)*, "I was at the party. I didn't see him leave. I didn't hear him scream or anything," like they were feeling guilty or something.

Who knows? To them, you're just another white shirt. To the undertaker, the mortician, the state trooper, your boss. Easily replaceable. Just one more for the road. But not to me. You were my world. And now you're gone. They forget that another white shirt leaves someone behind lonely. That he had a house and a car, and a wife and a kid. That he rode the same roads and elevators. That he paid the same taxes. That there's a hole in someone's life that no amount of tears or dirt will fill. They forget that they'll be just another white shirt someday, and their co-workers will be putting them to rest on some hot summer day in the middle of the week, or some mutually inconvenient time when some relative is sick, or out of town. When some attorney can't get everyone together to read the will.

It's getting dark. I have to leave before it gets dark. You know, it's hard to see.

(She hesitates, looks around as if to burn the image on her memory, tears up, starts to leave, and then remembers the flowers.)

Oh, I brought these for you.

This is for our first baby's birth. *(Throws one rose into the pool.)* This is for our second. *(Throws another.)* This is for our fifth anniversary. Our child's graduation from high school. *(Throws two.)* College graduations. *(One more.)* Your retirement. *(One more.)* Our first grandchild's birthday. *(One more.)* All the others. *(Three more.)* *(Pause, then she throws the last two.)* Our silver wedding anniversary. *(Silence.)* Our golden.

(She turns to leave.)

I have to leave. It's getting dark… It's getting… dark.

(She turns abruptly and exits stage left.)

(The lights fade on the rose waterfall, and then the stage goes dark.)

Lights down.

Scene 24

Lights up on STACY.

STACY

(She enters carrying three red roses left over from her prom corsage. She looks giddy as if she has a new boyfriend.)

I went to the senior prom, after all…with – you're never going to believe this, Chris M. We did an exchange day this year with their student council. And I keep seeing him in the mall. Yeah, I know, he dances like a geek. Worse than Elaine on Seinfeld. Way worse. *(She mimics the Elaine Dance)* Who else was I going to go with? There wasn't really anyone else. And you know we all switch it up anyway.

He was…nice. Came to the house in his parents' Mercedes. *That* was nice. My father managed to be absent. *(She absently rubs a spot on her neck. It's a hickey.)* Yeah, the band really sucked, but it was a good prom. Didn't get Prom Queen, but who knows who nominated me anyway? I think it was that snaggle-toothed old nun who runs the Library. I hated being on display. *(She rubs her neck.)*.

(She decides to share something with him, bends down, and whispers.) Yeah, we made out. I have to wear a turtleneck. For a while. *(Pause.)* They had a flask hidden under the coats. I didn't have any. I hate that smell.

We sort of tried to get together, but it didn't work out. You remember his dancing? Yeah, Remember when he used to do this really crazy dance in the middle of the floor and everybody loved it? He did it again at the prom. He was dancing crazy and he had no rhythm, yet somehow he pulled it off again. People pulled back in a circle to watch him. You know he's crazy. Crazy Chris. His eye still kind of goes off toward the side of his head. He's crazy. Yeah. He's not you…but I like him.

(She looks around, rubs her neck again absently and decides all of a sudden to go. She lays the roses on his grave and walks off.)

Lights down.

Scene 25

Lights up on SHARON.

(She is alone, without the baby, and she approaches TED's gravesite. She can't quite look at it, then she reaches out and rubs her fingertips over the dates inscribed on the stone. Suddenly, she becomes furious and kicks the gravestone, and then howls with pain.)

SHARON

Son of a bitch! *(She recovers from the blow.)* How could you do that to me? I just had the baby! We christened her on Sunday…I knew something was going on. You never came to me unless you wanted something. *(Pause)* Goddamn whore. I saw her in the bathrooms at work. In the hall. You fuck! Are ya happy now? Cause I sure am.

(She goes over to a bench positioned a slight distance away and sits. She takes out a cigarette

and lights it up, then takes a deep drag.)

(Refers to smoking) Yeah, I started. I'm rich, you know that? Richer than I ever could have been with you. They gave me a million and a half dollars. One-point-two after taxes, if you must know. That's what they said your lifetime earnings were worth. One point two. People are sending me shit all the time. Vacations, origami cranes, flags. *(Inhales deeply, then exhales. Coughs a bit.)* Yeah, I've even got Renee's college fund all set. I've got a promise for free tuition for four years! Paid off my law school debt. I'm Scott free, asshole. A new life, just me and my little daughter. She reminds me of what's important.

(She starts to inhale again, and then stops and throws the cigarette down to the ground and grinds it out with the toe of her shoe. Then she realizes she shouldn't litter, and picks up the butt.) She'll be better off without a lying thief of a daddy. Stole my youth. Yeah. That's right.

(She seems to remember the religious faith that has come into her life, falters in her attitude, and then decides she has to be true to herself. She stands.)

Yeah, we'll be much better off without you.

(She stops and looks at the grave marker, looks around, takes in the nice weather and sun, and decides to go.)

You pathetic fuck. Never could stand the heat... *(She starts to leave, then turns around)* How ironic! Here you are without me, and I have everything you ever wanted.

(SHARON exits.)

Lights down.

Scene 26
Spotlight on GHOST ANGEL.

(She is seated in her coffin as at the beginning of the play. She holds a red rose.)

("The Dance of the Heavenly White Shirts" is projected onto the scrim.)

We never had a child.

Funny. We come into this world and expect joy and we get grief.

And we leave this world in grief and we get joy…

(THE HEAVENLY DANCE OF THE WHITE SHIRTS begins. The lyric is, "We are in the dust")

(The entire company takes part in the dance. Each character iterates his or her special movement. The white shirts reappear from Scene 6, on the scrims.

The shirts gather like a tornado at the back of the stage and dance near the top of the proscenium, moving upstage and downstage and whirling all around. More and more light fills the stage. There is a tremendous wind. An image of a waterfall prevails. Fire [perhaps as light and sound] purifies each live character's soul. Each Spirit Dancer and the GHOST ANGEL guide the healing of the loved one whom he or she left behind. They also secondarily help the others and dance together. The image of the PLAYWRIGHT on video appears silently at the edge of the stage. She is breathing quietly and rhythmically. A small white shirt representing each of the living character's souls appears on the scrim. The PLAYWRIGHT starts to smile. ERICA, STACY, SHARON, and JUSTIN each find their own soul/shirt again and breathe it in. The lyric, "We are in the dust" crescendos, and then fades. The stage ends up full white light, purely joyful.)

(During the denouement, the music's time signature and phrasing changes so that it imitates the rhythm of breathing. This must happen gradually and there should be at least three minutes at the end of the play where the dancers are moving to the rhythm of "breathing" – an even four-count intake and an even four-count exhalation.)

(The men end the dance and remove themselves to the outer edges of the stage. The women finish the dance.)

(After the dance, one by one, they all go out into the audience again and whisper phrases of healing. The men speak as well now.)

(The phrases are:)

The sunbeam fell on your casket.
I felt…alive again.
I know you were there.
She reminds me of what's important.
That's what we agreed upon. For him.
I went to the senior prom after all.
I thought that it was worth it to go on.
And you know we all switch it up anyway.
He's not you…but I like him.
No matter what happens, your life is never perfect.
Grief leads to survival.

(They all move to the back of the auditorium and exit.)

END OF PLAY.

Short Plays – Comedy

THE DELIVERY

Development History

THE DELIVERY appeared in the Manhattan Shakespeare Project's 2010 Emerging Female Voices Festival. Twenty-one new works were presented around the theme of The Seven Ages of Man from AS YOU LIKE IT. THE DELIVERY appeared in the evening dedicated to The Infant. A staged reading was held on October 11, 2010 at Theaterlab in New York City. Lori Wolter Hudson directed.

FLOYD	Ian Michael Stuart
RALPH	Dartel McRae
CASSIE BERNHARDT	Erin Wilhelmi
MOTHER	Sally Cade Holmes

Characters

FLOYD	An Angel Messenger. The “good cop” figure.
RALPH	An Angel Messenger. The “bad cop” figure.
	They are big, tall, strong men in case there is any problem with the delivery.
CASSIE BERNHARDT	The delivery. Young, optimistic.
MOTHER	An image on a scrim who speaks in voiceover.

Place

Unit Set: The Celestial Subway, and the Delivery Room of a Hospital.

Time

Just before Birth, and Now.

(FLOYD, RALPH and CASSIE are riding on a subway. We see shadows indicating other "deliveries", most of whom are in groups of three.

CASSIE has a backpack that's filled to overflowing. RALPH is carrying it for her at the moment. CASSIE is fidgeting with her iPod.)

FLOYD

So let's go over this again. It's dark, you're swimming, and then BAM, you're out in the light and some bastard is smacking your ass.

RALPH

Try not to cry too much, or they'll give you some drug you'll never get off of.

CASSIE

Yeah, yeah, okay…

FLOYD

And when they hand you to your carrier, you say, "Thank you, Mater, I'm very pleased to meet you. Thank you for taking the delivery."

CASSIE

Yeah, okay.

FLOYD

See? I knew you weren't listening. Cassie, you cannot let on that you can speak, much less in 150 languages and 200 tribal dialects.

CASSIE

Dialects, schmialects. (*She pauses.*) Hey, do you think I'll remember them all by the time I apply to college? That'll really help my application.

FLOYD

No, you have to choose your language on this particular water marble. It's like citizenship. So you can have one, two countries – maybe five or six languages. You cannot keep all 350.

CASSIE

Well, I better have a good set of surrogates.

FLOYD

Cassie, you get what you get.

RALPH

No-one knows what the outcome will be. You always hope, but..

CASSIE

(Beginning to get scared) But what?

RALPH

Well, sometimes they're not what you expected. Sometimes… you only get one, or you get one who tries but really isn't any good at it.

CASSIE

Isn't good at surrogating? How hard can it be?

RALPH

At what they call "parenting"? Well, there are some basics, but…You see, they think that you belong to them.

CASSIE

What? I don't belong to anyone. I'm just on loan.

(FLOYD AND RALPH exchange a look.)

FLOYD

Umm, they always think they own you. Like they made you or something.

CASSIE

They just got to have a little fun while I downloaded.

FLOYD

Yeah, it's a little messed up when you think about it. They feel somehow, *powerful* when they get to be surrogates.

CASSIE

Well, I better get a good pair, because I am not going to be held back by anything.

FLOYD

Good girl, now hang on, we're going to have to jump off in a minute.

CASSIE

Alright. Look, why are there all those lights on down there? I can't even see my SG *(surrogate)* past all the people. How many of those pass-through things are there?

RALPH

They call them "doctors".

CASSIE

Oh, OK. Well, I don't remember having this many "doctors" before.

FLOYD

Let me take a look.

(*He examines the situation and looks back at her with a stricken look on his face.)*

Umm, Cassie, I have to tell you something. You're not the only one.

CASSIE

I'm not? Oooh, do I have a sister? Maybe it's Josie. Let me see.

FLOYD

No, Cassie. It seems your surrogate has overdone it. You're part of a multiple birth – an over-fertilization.

CASSIE

What the hell does that even mean?

FLOYD

It means you're not being delivered alone.

RALPH

Your carrier is a woman who likes to surrogate. A lot. Like a whole lot. Your carrier is …an Octomom.

CASSIE

(Pushes them aside to look over into the delivery room)

Oh, Hell, No! Let me see. *(She looks and then returns)*

FLOYD

Now, CAS…/

CASSIE

I am NOT going to be whelped like – what are those furry love-things?

RALPH

I think you mean a puppy.

CASSIE

I am not a puppy. I just finished a gig as a maharanee! I'm going to Barnard in exactly 17 years. Early decision.

Listen, I already have my world tour planned with my BFF Josie. We're going to Dubai and then over to Tahiti for a few weeks. Stay in Marlon Brando's old house, it's an eco-spa now, you know. Spring Break, two thousand…

RALPH

It might not work out that way.

FLOYD

But it might –

CASSIE

Nooo! I'm going back.

RALPH

(Taking on the strong-arm role.)

You're not going back.

(He blocks her.)

FLOYD

Alright, we're getting ready to jump. Come on. It'll be OK.

(Cassie p*repares to jump. She takes one strap of the backpack.)*

FLOYD and RALPH

Ready, set, go. *(They act as if they're all jumping, but they let Cassie go by herself at the last minute.)*

CASSIE
(Looking up.)

Good bye, good bye.

(She descends into a sea of bright lights. She feels someone smack her hard on her bottom.)

Hey, knock it off. Oh, right, they told me not to cry.

(She holds on to her bottom and looks up onto a scrim with a blurred image of a woman's face)

Hey, hello. How are you? Good afternoon. My name is…

MOTHER *(in voiceover)*
Yes, that's right, Waaah, waaah. My little sweetie pie.

CASSIE
No, not wah. I said, "Good afternoon". Didn't anyone ever teach you manners?

MOTHER *(V.O.)*
Mommy's going to put you over there with all your brothers and sisters.

CASSIE
Look, this may not be the best time, but I need to talk to you about something. I do not want to be raised in a litter with all those other downloads. I

need to go to Barnard. You're just going to have to take care of the payment. I'll try to get a job, do some work... *(She doubles over in pain as the doctor snips her umbilical cord.)* Agghhh, oh, you're killing me! That hurts, you stupid mask face! Haven't you heard of anesthesia?

MOTHER *(V.O.)*
That's all right, baby, Mommy will give you something to eat.

(CASSIE feels herself being lifted into MOTHER'S arms.)

(MOTHER is smothering her)

CASSIE
Hey, what the hell is this thing? It's like a big lard ball. You're choking me, get it off me, take it away!

MOTHER (*in voiceover)*
Don't you want any milk? Here, try again, baby, what's wrong?

CASSIE
There is nothing wrong, you idiot, can't you see you're choking me? Lay off! What the hell is wrong with you? *(She composes herself.)* As I was saying, you need to send me to private school, Spence, not Dalton – to prepare me…

MOTHER *(V.O.)*

She doesn't want any milk.

CASSIE

(Lifts her arm and gets tagged with a name bracelet. She looks at a "tag" on her wrist)

JANICE? No, my name is not Janice, "Mother". My name is CASSIE. CASS-SEE. You are exhausting me.

MOTHER *(V.O.)*

Mommy is going to take care of you and keep you safe and love you until the day you die....

CASSIE

Oh, right, about that? I'm only here for a little while, anyway. Just do the basics – feed me, don't make me fat, save your money, and send me to... (*She hears someone offstage speaking a rare Roman dialect.)* What? Really? There are a few of you from where? Oh, I've been there, one of my past lives, five cycles ago. *(She listens.)* Yeah, I liked it. Look, I can't come over there. This monstrosity seems to like holding me. I guess I'm the last to be delivered. *(She's starting to chew on something. It's her scarf which she's treating like a baby blanket.)* Yeah, Ralph and Floyd. You know them, too? Good. Oh, wait, wait, I know how to get over there. I'll act like I'm sleepy.

MOTHER *(V.O.)*

Is little Janice sleepy? Mummy will send her over to be with her little baby brothers and sisters.

CASSIE

Yeah, yeah, just get me the transport. (*To herself.*) Maybe this won't be so bad. *(She straightens her clothing and squares off against MOTHER.)* But you better not fuck this up, Big Thing. Food, clothing, shelter, and love. Yeah, LOVE. Deliveries need it – for some reason. Just remember, I came into this world and I can take myself right out of it again. So you better get it right the first time. Right. Now get those damn lights out of my eyes or give me a pair of sunglasses.

(The lights dim suddenly.)

CASSIE

All right. That's more like it. Now give me a lift. I want to meet the rest of the brood.

(CASSIE picks up her backpack and slings it over her shoulders. She's ready to start her new life. The lights dim.)

(She looks at her mother, in a threatening way, one more time.)

Remember. *Spence*. Not Dalton. Alright, now take me over there.

(She "relaxes" into her mother's arms like she's the Queen of Sheba.)

(Lights down.)

END OF PLAY.

Short Plays – Drama

MARIA, THE DAY AFTER

A Short, Non-Musical Sequel to WEST SIDE STORY

Development History

The playwright read MARIA, THE DAY AFTER at the NO PASSPORT/Hibernating Rattlesnakes event on January 25, 2010 at the Nuyorican Poets Café in New York City. She also read THE LAST STONE – OR, THE ADULTERESS SPEAKS FOR HERSELF and "Haiti Calling" that evening.

Characters

MARIA	The young woman.
HERNANDO	Her father.

Setting

The bedroom where Maria made love to Tony the night before.

Place
New York City.

Time
The day after the Rumble.

(There are video screens of varying sizes in different parts of the stage. Prominently, there is one which will give a close-up of her face as she goes through the following memories and emotions. Another screen, smaller and in a less prominent place, comes on and pictures her father after he leaves the room. This one will portray a father's control over his daughter's life and sexuality.)

(Music: There are snippets of phrases from ***WEST SIDE STORY****, particularly trumpets from the fight scene when she is remembering Tony dead on the ground. The music can include new compositions, as long as it provides an underlying impression of the musical phrases from* ***WEST SIDE STORY*** *as Maria goes through her memories. The new music should create a new construct for Maria's processing of the events of the last 24 hours. These musical memories should become part of the emotional construction of her thoughts for her future. At the end, the music and video cuts out so that we hear only her sobs in the silence.)*

(Lights: The lights should remain simple and evoke her mental and emotional memory.)

(Action: It is dawn. Maria has been up all night long. Her parents are crying and screaming in the next room. She is afraid, yet she is lying in the bed where she made love with Tony the night before, and she is filled with memories of his scent and his body. She is thinking of him and touching herself

and having an orgasm.)

(Suddenly the noise stops next door. We hear her moaning and see her writhing underneath the blankets.)

(Her father bursts into the room and stares at her. He doesn't comprehend what she's doing, writhing under the blankets and moaning. He thinks she's grieving the death of her brother.)

(She doesn't know he's there.)

HERNANDO
(Screams)
Do you know what you've done to my family?

She throws back the blankets and looks at him, wide-eyed.

He walks over to her bed, stands over her and looks at her intently. He spits on her. And then he leaves.

She is stunned and lies there for awhile, humiliated.

She remains silent and stares into space.

Then we see all of the following on her face, but she says nothing.

She remembers making love to Tony.

She thinks of Tony lying on the ground, dead, and feels the warm steel of the gun in her hands.

For two beats, her face and body register this memory.

A cry escapes her lips.

She thinks of her brother Bernardo, dead – and how they'll have to prepare a funeral for him.

Does she have anything black to wear?

She thinks of Anita telling her that her brother is dead.

She feels betrayed by Tony. This bothers her more than anything and she doesn't know why.

She thinks of her childhood in Puerto Rico with Bernardo – the sun and the heat, the beach, avocados, smells of her mother's cooking, playing.

She wonders if her parents will still make her marry Chino.

For two beats, her face and body registers her thoughts on this question.

She realizes that she'll never make love again. She'll never trust – and never experience love, which is life – again.

She fears that her grief will last forever.

She starts to cry, with heaving sobs.

Lights down.

END OF PLAY.

MORE THAN LIFE ITSELF

Characters

MAN	20-something, dressed in a well-made suit and tie, all decked out with wires, carrying coffee, and seeming to be jumpy.
WOMAN	Any age, wearing older-style clothing, slightly disheveled.

Place

Unit Set: Bryant Park, NYC – S.R.

Union Square Park, NYC – S.L.

Time

The present.

(Lights up on two parks. The characters sit on opposite sides of the stage facing downstage right and downstage left respectively. The MAN is upstage right, and facing downstage left. The WOMAN is downstage left, facing downstage right. The MAN is sitting near the fountain in Bryant Park in the middle of the work day. He is talking on phone headset. The cords dangle down and are tucked into his suit. He can get up and walk around as he gets more agitated during the scene, but must be seated just before the line, "I will, you dog hater." The WOMAN is sitting on a bench near the dog run in Union Square Park. Sounds of dogs barking, children playing, and buses.)

MAN

I *told* you I don't want you to do that when I'm not home.

(WOMAN *nods head.)*

MAN

When did he get out?

WOMAN

One o'clock.

MAN

How long was he out?

WOMAN

About twenty minutes…

MAN

You didn't go look for him?

WOMAN

I knew he'd come back. You weren't out there. I knew he'd just run around and come back.

MAN *(increasingly agitated)*

But he could have gotten lost or stolen. What is *wrong* with you? You know I love that dog more than life itself.

WOMAN *(Repeats)*

More than life…I *didn't* think…I didn't …*think*…

MAN

Yeah, you *didn't* think! I am never going to leave my dog in your care again. Never.

WOMAN

Suit yourself.

(Silence while the man broods. Pause.)

WOMAN

Well, what else is new?

MAN *(Sarcastically)*

Nothing. Absolutely nothing.

WOMAN *(These next few lines overlap.)*
You don't have to be like that.../

MAN
Like *that*! You nearly kill my dog and I'm "like that." I'm going to go!

WOMAN
All right, suit yourself.

MAN
Yeah, you said that already, I *will*, you dog hater!

(*He springs to his feet.)*

(WOMAN *clucks her tongue, rolls her eyes and hangs up with a deliberate motion.)*

(When the MAN springs up, the wires to his earpiece swing forward to reveal that there is no phone attached to the earpiece. He has no phone. The MAN stands in a defiant and lonely position facing downstage. The WOMAN sits still for a moment at this point. Then she shrugs her shoulders and heads off for the dog park.)

(The dog run is indicated by sound and light, and dogs' shadows. The sound of barking grows louder. Something off right catches the MAN's attention and his head snaps towards it. Then he briskly exits S.R.)

(Blackout.)

(The sound of the dogs' barking crescendos, then fades to nothing.)

END OF PLAY.

Monologues for Women – Drama

AND THEN I WENT INSIDE

Kathleen Chalfant as Stacy Lee Madison in AND THEN I WENT INSIDE. Miss Chalfant premiered the role at the League of Professional Theatre Women's 2009 New Play Festival, held at the Cherry Lane Theatre in New York City.

(Photo by Gerry Goodstein)

AND THEN I WENT INSIDE

Production History

This play premiered in an AEA-approved benefit performance by and for the League of Professional Theatre Women entitled "2009 New Play Festival - Turning Points: Women Have Their Say" on November 9, 2009 at the Cherry Lane Theatre in New York City.

Co-Producers: Joan D. Firestone and Rachel Reiner.

STACY LEE MADISON Kathleen Chalfant.

Bouquet designed and built by Anne Hamilton.

Director: Lorca Peress; Festival Scenic Designer: Kina Park; Festival Lighting Designer: Pamela Kupper; Festival Sound Designer: Joanna Lynne Staub; Half Light Sound Designer: Marcelo Anez; Festival Stage Manager: Hannah Perryman; Assistant Stage Manager: Geoffrey Nixon; Lighting Assistant: Flora Vassar; Production Assistant: Sean McCain; Program Design: Faye Armon; Tickets: DeVida Jenkins.

Dedicated to the memory of Curtis Nurnberger.

Development History

The playwright portrayed the role of Stacy in a staged reading of AND THEN I WENT INSIDE on March 26th, 27th and 28th, 2010 at the Shubin Theatre in Philadelphia. The readings were part of a benefit for Green Light Arts.

AND THEN I WENT INSIDE appeared as PART II of THE STACY PLAY – A LOVE SONG – VOLUME I in TRANSITIONS, a international juried Virtual Exhibit at Pen and Brush, one of the oldest and most prestigious women's arts collectives in America. The exhibit appeared online from June 3rd through September 3rd, 2010 and a copy was available for reading at Pen and Brush at 16 East 10th Street in New York City. The exhibit also included the author's full-length play ANOTHER WHITE SHIRT and her poem, "Gondolier".

AND THEN I WENT INSIDE appeared as PART II of THE STACY PLAY – A LOVE SONG – VOLUME I in a staged reading in the New York City home of legendary American producer Julia Miles on December 14, 2010. Julia's Reading Room is a program of the League of Professional Theatre Women. The playwright directed the reading and Haley Ward read the stage directions.

STACY	Anne Hamilton
JONATHAN	Christopher Gliege

The playwright read an excerpt from AND THEN I WENT INSIDE at the Philadelphia Writer's Conference in June, 2011.

AND THEN I WENT INSIDE

A Bouquet, A Flying Teen, and One Lover too Many

Character

STACY is 55 years old, an artist and a scholar.

THE BOUQUET - The bouquet is a very important part of Part II. It's the second character. Stacy makes a piece of art while she tells us about her life. The bouquet must be beautiful and well-designed, and its scale must be appropriate so that it can be seen clearly from any seat in the house.

Setting

Stacy's desk and chair, her couch, and an easel with a painting she's working on. The painting is covered with a drape.

Place

Stacy's apartment on the Upper West Side of Manhattan.

Time

2009

But at my back I always hear
Time's wingèd chariot hurrying near;
And yonder all before us lie
Deserts of vast eternity.

-Andrew Marvell
From *To His Coy Mistress*

(Lights up on a fifty-five-year-old woman. Gray hair has just begun to frame her face. She sits at a table drinking a glass of water as the lights come up. She's making a piece of art. She's arranging small items that the audience can't see, making two piles, one on the left and one on the right. There is a bouquet of flowers on her left which is beautifully made of beads and wire. It is almost a full bouquet. She is working on the last flower.)

(She places the glass of water on her right. A bed or couch covered with messy piles of blankets and pillows sits upstage right. The bedding should be elegant. A painting on an easel half covered with a drape sits upstage left. She addresses the audience as she works.)

STACY

I just realized that I've been in love with a dead man for forty years.

(Beat)

Well, a dead teenager. Who knows if he was a man yet? Yeah. Forty long years, in love with a ghost. My high school lover. Did anyone have lovers back then? I guess I did. As close to real love as possible. A big, tall, he-man bear-hugging, tight-assed teenager. Who drank. And smoked. And loved everyone he ever met.

(She takes up a couple of beads from the pile on the

left, threads them on a wire, then takes a small item which we can't see and places it on the right side of the table.)

"What happened?" Well you may ask. Car accident. On a nice June afternoon. Right on the highway near the mall. On the highway – a pothole. It sat – or dipped there – right at the light where the guard rail ended. And when he drove by, BAM, bloop, skip. It hopped, skipped and jumped him right into the path of a tractor trailer.

BAM, skip, jump. He flew from the car. No one wore a seatbelt back then.

BAM, sail, fly. Wind shearing off his ears (not that they were big). Birds looking down in amazement. "What is this big, bear-y thing in our airspace?" I'll bet they looked down their yellow bird- beaky noses and said, "I disapprove. I'm definitely going to call the city about this one. Bears in the sky. Goddamn taking up our airspace." *(Beat, and then she looks directly at the audience.)* People aren't supposed to fly.

(She threads a bead on a piece of wire. Then she takes a small item from the left of her table and starts to make a pile on the right.)

(Beat. She smiles.)

Here's my pile. I like to…pile things. To pile them

up and watch so they don't fall over. Make sure they sit still. It's like a game. When the pile FALLS, it's over. *(Beat)* Balance. Yeah. Balance is important.

(She examines her work and finds it in good order.)
Yeah, piles.

(Looks at the audience. Screws up her courage. She wants to tell the whole story.)

So let's begin again.

So I'm a Catholic schoolgirl, daughter of a wanna-be nun who met a man who looked like Clark Gable and fell in love. So much for chastity. Working class household. Cold house in the winter. Dusty. Bad neighborhood. German shepherd protects us from the neighbors.

Brother on the track team. Always won medals, never shared his triumphs. Working class.

(She shakes her head.)

I said that. Springsteen. New Jersey. Pollution. Enough said.

School play. The musical. I'd been cheated out of the lead in my own school play, so I went over to my brother's all-boy's school. Same musical. WEST SIDE STORY. I got the lead.

A funny, tall guy starts talking to me. He had a lot of curly hair. We were doing our acting warm-ups.

"Hey, are you Madison's sister?" "Yes, I am." "I can't believe it."

I look at him quizzically. He smiles, and I'm a goner. That's all it took.

So - Rehearsals, opening night, closing, cast party, tears.

"It's over," I cry. "We'll see each other again, in the mall," he says. He comforts me.

His parents go to Argentina during Spring Break. He throws a party. We all stand around drinking beer and looking at each other. I help him with the food. I have to leave early. My parents are over-protective.

We go to the prom together. We take pictures. He doesn't even try to put his hands on my ass during the slow dance.

(She thinks about this, and strings another few beads on the wire. She twists the wire - she's making a flower with leaves. There's a pile of already completed wire and bead flowers to her left on the table. She puts a few more small items in the pile on her right.)

I feel – a little off-kilter. Like something inside is

falling over. Slipping.

Yeah, so he invites me to his graduation. He failed math and has to go to summer school, but they let him go through the ceremony anyway. Cost his parents enough to send him there. They would have pitched a fit.

(Beat)

He should have said something. I would have helped him. He was going to college anyway. He didn't care.

(Beat)

Freedom.

But I have to stay home because I have to take care of the house while my parents work. I read, cook, play with the dog. Try to get a tan, but the sun isn't strong enough yet.

Ten days after the ceremony. He calls – we talk three times a day anyway – "Do you want to come to the movies?" "I can't." "Come on. We'll be back before your mother gets home." "I can't."

"All right. I'll go by myself. Love you."

(Incredulously)

Love you. And he hangs up. I feel good. And strange.

(Now she gets agitated, and starts piling on the beads quicker. After five or so, she stops and moves five small items from the left side of her table to the right side.)

That did it. City cops said that other people had died at that intersection, and it was a state road. The city couldn't fix it. They just kept an eye on it. Yeah, blueshirt. An eye. Like a fucking bird's eye, looking straight into my boyfriend's face while he was flying through the air?

(Stops)

Oh, right. He wasn't my boyfriend. We never – got together.

They said they'd fix it – the pothole – when enough people died at the intersection. They fixed it right after him. (*She pauses to reflect.)* Fucking pathetic grownups. *(Beat.)* I didn't care. I just wanted my friend back.

"Stand on your own two feet," my father said. "You'll be alright."

"Stacy Lee is just not herself," said my favorite aunt. Do yuh *think*? Someone's here, and then someone's gone. And not just one of the guys. My guy.

Well, he wasn't *really* my guy.

(This statement seems to bother her. She doesn't put any more beads on the wire. She just takes a small pile of items from the left and puts them on the right.)

So I started making piles. They looked like I felt inside. Slippery, and…shifty. Like everything could fall over at any minute.

(She indicates with her hand off toward the right and the left, and forward, at different levels, to indicate the bed, the sink, the leaves, etc.)

I put them on my bed – piles of clothes. In the kitchen, piles of dishes. Outside, piles of leaves I was supposed to pick up. My mother was mad, but what could she say?

In English class, a pile of papers on my desk - there was no room to take notes - couldn't fit a notebook there. So I just stared into Sister Mary Evangeline's forehead, acting like I was trying to memorize every word. She never caught on.

In gym class, I'd wait 'til the teacher went into the locker room, then pile all the volleyball nets into one big mess. I never got into trouble for it. I was an A-plus student. Of course. No disorder there. Class, home, one activity, perfect grades.

(She looks down at her wire flower, and measures it against the others. It is almost finished. She finishes

it up during the next section.)

So I graduate. Go to college. Top of my class, except for first semester junior year when I couldn't get out of bed. *(Reflects.)* Nothing bad can happen to you when you're hiding under a pile of covers. *(Then, bitterly.)* That little problem kept me out of Phi Beta Kappa. *(Beat.)* Off to Oxford. I study the philosophy of aesthetics – what is beautiful, and why? Actually, I learned…that art does not have to be beautiful. Art … can be raw, just like life. *(She shrugs.)* Aesthetics. Impractical, but why not?

I get out of school, get out of Jersey. Work two or three jobs, trying to make ends meet. Hours in the studio, I paint and take my stuff to the gallery. I move out to the Island. The First Guy A-H – After –Him – was a blond with blue eyes. Tall guy. Funny, everybody loves him. I would have died for this guy. I'm infatuated and want to get married. But he takes off – just moves out of his apartment and runs.

It turns out he's gay. I get pneumonia and end up in bed again and almost die. *(Beat)* Almost did.

Something's slipping. I can't keep my piles straight. That fear of "What if something bad happens today and I can't deal with it?" The anxiety is killing me.

So I move to the city and go out with another guy - He's the second guy A-H. This is seven years later.

It turns out he's a millionaire. Well, a millionaire's *son.* And not just one million. A hundred freaking million. He looks like Michelangelo's David.

(Beat)

My career's taking off. I win a fellowship. Off to Paris – a residency. I meet a writer. A genius. Hmmm. *(She's thinking about him.)*

We fall in love. We want to get married. He's got a girlfriend. Promises me he'll break up with her. We spend the weekend in bed, then he decides he doesn't want to let her go just yet. She's supporting him. He now wants me to support him while he *(She throws her hands in the air and waves them around in an airy way)* makes up stories. *(Beat).* What about *my* art, *my* career? *(Beat)* When he leaves this time, I give him the Madison Kiss of Death. Yeah, you know what that is? *(As if to him)* "Thank you for coming. I love you."

And in my heart I'm saying, "Thank you for coming into my life. I love you more than you will ever know. But no more." And I give him a beautiful kiss. *(Beat)* And then I went inside. *(Beat)* Disconnect the phone. *(She says, as if to him-)* "Go back to fucking Chicago, you jerk!" Then I get under the piles of blankets and don't come out. *(Beat.)* It's easy to keep your balance on a bed. For a while.

(She wraps the bead flowers with a red ribbon. It looks like a bouquet that you'd place on a grave. She picks up a card and starts writing on it, then looks at her pile on the right and counts it out silently, but we can't see the items. This can take a moment. She gathers her items into a pile again.)

(She picks up the card and writes a few words on it as she speaks this last bit.)

There was a Lithuanian. Messy hair like Sting, biggest dick I've ever seen. Separated. He didn't want to get into another relationship right away. *(She looks up and rolls her eyes.)*

The pro basketball player. *(She keeps writing.)* Mmmmmmm. Six foot seven, shaved head, espresso-dark skin. Lovely! *(Now she's writing something on the card painstakingly and slowly.)* He wanted a place to live 'til he could decide whether to go back and play for the Knicks. *(She shakes off the memory.)*

(Now she's writing quickly, finishing off her card.)

Lastly, that little Turkish shit who had a wife and kid back in Ankara. Fuck. Me.

(She carefully examines the card. She straightens the items on her work desk. Straightens the bouquet. Places the remainder of the beads back in a small jar.)

(She holds the card up and reads its words aloud.) "To everyone who ever really cared about me. I love you more than you will ever know. I'm tired of making piles. They always fall over anyway. I couldn't keep it all together. Sorry. Stacy."

(She kisses the card, and tucks it under the red ribbon on the bouquet. It's clear that there's something else going on in her head. She's giving it the Madison Kiss of Death.)

(She pushes the little items from the right of the table to the center. She picks up the glass of water and toasts the audience. We finally see that she's got a pile of pills on the table. She starts to take them, methodically, one by one, doing a ritual. She takes one, drinks a sip of water, takes two, sips water, takes three, sips water, then takes four and sips water. Then she shrugs, and takes a handful, very neatly and in a feminine manner and finishes off the water. She may repeat this action. She has now taken all the pills.)

(She once more straightens items on the table and picks up the bouquet. She shrugs again. There's no self-pity here.) The philosophy of aesthetics…I believe that every life is a work of art.

(She turns around, walks over to the canvas and removes the drape from the painting. She returns to the table, picks up the bouquet and goes to the bed.

She places the bouquet on top of the blankets and gets underneath them completely. She can't be seen anymore. She's just part of the pile now and can't be distinguished. Perhaps her hand holding the bouquet lies on top of the blanket. A spotlight hits the bouquet. Lights slowly fade.)

(Blackout.)

END OF PLAY.

RED RIBBON TIE

Development History

RED RIBBON TIE appears as scenes 4, 9 and 13 in ANOTHER WHITE SHIRT, which is published in this volume. The role was first read in the New York City home of legendary American producer Julia Miles on April 6, 2009. Julia's Reading Room is a program of the League of Professional Theatre Women. The playwright directed the reading.

ERICA	Erika Iverson
MARY (later named STACY)	Stacy Davidowitz
SHARON	Rachel Murdy
GHOST ANGEL	Margi Sharp Douglas

Alissa Hunnicut read the role of the PLAYWRIGHT and the stage directions.

RED RIBBON TIE appeared as scenes 4, 9 and 13 in ANOTHER WHITE SHIRT in TRANSITIONS, an international juried Virtual Exhibit. The exhibit was created by Pen and Brush, one of the oldest and most prestigious women's arts collectives in America. The playwright read the three monologues at the opening in Manhattan on June 3, 2010. Her works appeared online from June 3rd through September 3rd, 2010 and copies were available for reading at Pen and Brush at 16 East 10th Street in New York City. The exhibit also included the author's full-length play THE STACY PLAY – A LOVE SONG – VOLUME I and her poem, "Gondolier".

The playwright read RED RIBBON TIE at the Philadelphia Writer's Conference in June, 2011.

Character

SHARON, 27 years old, worked as an attorney in Tower One of the World Trade Center. She is a World Trade Center Widow and survivor of the attacks.

Place

SHARON's Living Room in Forest Hills, New York

Time

September 13, 2001

(It is Thursday, September 13, 2001 at 8:46 a.m. Sharon is at home in Forest Hills, Queens, New York. We see something next to her wrapped in a blanket, but we don't know what it is at first. It turns out to be her baby, Renee. She's rocking back and forth.)

(She is very sad, to the point of death.)

SHARON

When the first plane hit it knocked the coffee right out of my mug. I had worked all week on that document and I lost it . My computer just shorted out. I started cursing, then I smelled the fuel - the rush of the explosion and the jet fuel. I couldn't believe it. What was happening?

The heat made my wedding ring burn on my finger. I tried to rip it off but it just wouldn't come. It was like I had a fire of molten glass on my finger. Or gasoline. The fuel. And the Smell. Of – what – of steel being burned, exploded and then I was drinking it. Like some big fire eater, I felt it ignite my lipstick, singe off my taste buds, pass my jaws and settle. In the back of the throat. A searing beak nipping off my tonsils, and down my esophagus, melting every organ in its path, and to the top of my lungs, like a glassblower nipping off a stem. I thought, "My lungs are going to go, they're going to fly around in there, where will they go?" And then my cilia, scorching, steaming into nothing hair by hair, with patterns waving like a bonfire, waving in the breeze, stuck. Struck by fire. It was over, I thought, I can't stand this pain. It must be...over. Others, I saw them sitting there, calling people on their cell phones, joking. They thought they had time.

(Pause.)

I ran to find you - down the hall, two doors to the right. They were hot to the touch. People were screaming. I saw my boss – well, his chair, melted. I could barely look at it, there was so much smoke. I ran through the conference room, to your desk. Your chair was thrown back, I fought to get through – another hot door, hot ashes gluing to my face. The fires. The papers...on...

I felt a hot wind and thought, oh, thank God, I can get some fresh air, I'm dying. I rounded the corner and found you. Ted! Ted! Right on the edge – you were on the edge of the window, and all I could see was a shadow, with...arms...and heels. Her arms on you, reaching, and you reaching back. She was crying. And you held her. You. Held. Her...I stopped and stared. No words could come… And you took her hand...I said...what?...? *(Pause... Pause... Pause).* And you jumped.

(Looks off into the distance for a beat in horror.)

(Red and white fire truck lights grow softly at "My feet were burning..." and then build. At the end,

they are at full strength as if she is running past a fire truck. Then they cut off at her last word "dark" when she blacks out.)

And. You. Jumped. Off the window ledge, the broken, twisted metal. I rushed to the edge and cut my feet on the glass – You looked like an upside down balloon, floating headfirst...softly through the ashes, down, down, down into the ground...Your suit billowing rippling out, that...dark shadow pasted to your side. Like a sideshow attraction I couldn't take my eyes off. Down, softly, the round balloon, like Renee's little panda balloons... all black and white and those red ribbons around their necks. Your tie, tinier and tinier, like a red ribbon around your neck, and then I couldn't see you anymore.

The fear began to build and I ran to find you. "I'll catch him on the other end!" I'll take the express elevator and go downstairs and catch him before he hits the ground. I just have to – run. I have to run. So I took my shoes off and started running – slammed the elevator button. No elevator. My feet were burning...Hot and sharp, glass in my toes and still I ran – red exit signs, how many stairs for each floor? Hot. Couldn't touch the walls, breathing sharp and knees ache, feet pounding. Like moles feeling their way along a tunnel. Not touching, touching, others, lemmings running off the cliff together, railing stick to railing, countless, flat steps, jumping up to meet me, pounding, no rest until my lungs explode. Again, to run, no time and then some air, some light a fireman pulling me down and pulling away, away through dust and light and fire and off to find the arms, a shadow, black and white, ballooning, red ribbon tie, I found you. Catch you. I'll catch you now. A shadow coming closer, down like light blown up into the sky's horizon, catch you. Catch you and shadow and catch you some shadow and you you you see you catch and then the dark....

(Lights out suddenly as SHARON loses consciousness.)

END OF PLAY.

HEART TALK

A Certified Letter to Richard White, Head Evangelist and C.F.O. of the Church of Our Lord Jesus Christ and His Disciples in the City of New York, Inc.

Character

MARCY MARSDEN-COOPER, A professor, early-30's. She has a strong determined jaw line, yet a softness that exposes a sensitive soul.

Place

Marcy's one-bedroom apartment in Chelsea, NYC. Books on cheap shelves surround her. She sits in a cheap swivel chair. A large calendar is tacked to the wall to the right side of her desk.

Time

1990

(Lights up on Marcy seated at her desk. She is making some calculations using a calculator and counting dates on a calendar stuck on the wall. A pile of papers on the desk make up the Certified Letter. She reads from the letter she is writing. From time to time she makes notes as she speaks. After a bit, she addresses Richard White directly, as if he is sitting before her.)

MARCY

To Richard White, Head Evangelist and C.F.O. of the Church of Our Lord Jesus Christ and His Disciples in the City of New York, Inc.

This is what I gave your church: six years, nine months and twenty one days of my thirty-one-year-old life.

Six years and nine months of space in my apartment for your Bible studies, 2000 miles worth of rides in my car.

Almost all the hours I spent outside of school and work. 4,872 meals. And $23,450.25 in cash.

(Beat)

I want it all back.

This is what your people took from me without my permission:

One Evan Picone classic navy suit jacket; one brand new answering machine; One Eddie Bauer trench coat, down lining (useless) left behind; one handmade tartan blanket I bought for myself and carried by hand from northern Scotland; one tape recorder, handed off through a church leader to a member who skipped out after a few weeks. The "leader" didn't even offer to pay for it.

Not to mention my frying pan. My mother bought me that frying pan – new, non-stick, perfect for bacon and eggs. And there it was – scratched and ruined. I want it all back.

I had…faith…before I started up with you. A wandering faith, yes – I was Catholic, Baptist, a Fundamentalist. A college friend invited me to your services. I was 23 and just on my own for the first time after college. They told me later that you…preyed… on young people who'd just left home for the first time. Set out to separate them from their families, get them to follow you.

That you "love bombed" them, having your people show all kinds of attention and affection to sort of trick them into believing you cared, that they'd found a new home.

That's pretty clever, faking out another organism by pretending to harmonize with it. Sort of like how a chameleon changes its colors to escape detection. Yeah, escaping detection, that was another trick. You systematically broke down bridges between the individual, say, Exhibit A, and the rest of her life.

"You can't trust your parents," you preached from the pulpit, "Follow Jesus. Take up your cross and follow me." Yeah, I took up your cross – YOUR cross, not the Lord's. Your housing costs, your cell phone bill, your travel to distant parts of the world to meet with your cohorts trying to *save humanity.* You advised us to live four or five to a two bedroom apartment, give all our non-essential money to the church, spend time building the church instead of our careers, our jobs, our vocations, our lives.

You *look* like the picture of health. "Happy" families, loving partnerships – only heterosexual, of course – that's what you *say* makes up the church. God knows how many gay people you married off to "straighten them out" in your words.

(Now it's as if she is addressing Richard White directly.)

I wonder what went on behind your closed doors – the violence you did to your wife. What made you so hateful? And make no mistake, violence done to someone else is always violence done to yourself. It must have hurt – something deep inside – to make you tell others they were going to hell and they needed you to stop them. And then the diversion of sacredness. You inserted one degree of separation between each person and her life – putting yourself in the place of Christ – of the enlightened soul, the enlightened Being who preached peace and love and honesty. You couldn't fill his shoes, why even try?

Disgust. That's all I have for you, you pathetic losers. Tramps, vagabonds, moving across the country as soon as someone finds you out. Somebody's going to shoot you on the sidewalk someday for what you did to them. It's wrong to force a belief system on anyone. Always on the run from mistreating human beings and your own children. That's right, your own children.

How many competitive miscarriages happened on your watch? Yeah, that's what I said, you know what I'm talking about. It became a badge of honor. You used your wife to put pressure on pregnant women to run around in all kinds of weather without proper nutrition or rest, serving the church. No slowing down, no concern for their health. Doctors ordered bed rest but they said, "The Lord will take care of it." Yeah, well, the Lord took care of it. He took his unborn babies home because he knew you'd probably fuck up their little lives for the sake of your tiny little sense of self-worth. You couldn't live a decent life from the inside out and you made sure that no-one else even got the most basic chance.

(She takes a deep breath.)

When I started at NYU, I didn't even have enough money to eat. I was trying to keep up with all of the services all over the city, that was when you had to pay $1.50 each time you took a bus or subway. I was trying to study, and you insisted on having inane college study groups where we sat around for an hour singing freaking Jesus songs like we were kids at a campfire.

All those stupid, useless Friday night meetings. I needed to study – to go to class, to go to symposia, that's what I was there for. I moved to the city to go to a top notch university and to make something of myself. You insisted that I contribute to the missions, the church, the collection to plant a church somewhere in some faraway city.

I made $150 a week. I had no savings. My monthly rent was $450. I had sold out to get this amazing education. I didn't have money for food – ate apples I bought from a street vendor for 25 cents, ramen noodles, of course, and bagels everyday because they filled me up for $1.00. Do you know I couldn't even look at a bagel or an apple for ten years after I graduated?

Listen to this, Dick: One night, at a Bible study in the apartment of a church leader, we'll call her, Exhibit A – the apartment which I helped pay for with my contribution money – I told the woman I was hungry and she flipped. "Why aren't you handling your money better?" she demanded. I can still see the daggers coming out of her eyes. If she could have gotten away with spitting on me, she would have. "You need to get more focused on the kingdom of God. You don't have your priorities straight! You're supposed to give to the church." We were in her kitchen. I told her that I wasn't making enough money to live properly with only a work study job at $10 an hour. She clucked her tongue with disgust, pulled a chair out, climbed on top of it, reached into an upper cabinet and pulled down a box of pasta and a couple of jars of sauce. *(wondrously)* She had extra food! She shoved them into my arms – no bag – and snarled, "Do better next time." *(Pause and then softly)* I took the food. I needed to eat.

She had a puppy, Exhibit B, a yellow lab named Libby. It was a beautiful young dog. She kept it locked in her room while she was out “saving people”. It chewed through the door, she was always screaming at it. It was a perfectly wonderful puppy.

She was going out with another popular leader – a real catch in terms of church status, you know who I’m talking about. Said she was practicing taking care of a dog so she would be ready to be a mother after they got married. A mother, huh? If you can’t treat an animal properly, how can you possibly treat a human baby well?

This was the same bitch who got married and went to Tahiti for three weeks with her new husband and then moved into a bigger apartment as soon as she got back. Three weeks of honeymoon. Where did they get the money for that? They were both ministers for your church.

Did their families give it to them? The rest of us were systematically cut off from our families, told they couldn’t be trusted. Why were they still close to their families and on such good terms that their Moms and Dads would actually bankroll an expensive honeymoon? You pressured the rest of us every week to increase our contributions, and no joke – to give ten times our regular weekly contribution to the Special Collection every summer. Did *I* pay for her honeymoon, Rich? Special collection - It was a goal to be met and we –

I – met it every year. Against all hope, the Lord provided, yes, through *my* faith, and that was a miracle.

All you church leaders who married one another did that – went off on long honeymoons, so you must have had resources YOU didn't liquidate like the rest of us. Or you didn't sacrifice fully and actually held something back. *(Beat.)* How can you impoverish someone else for your own gain? You all lived in beautiful buildings in good neighborhoods. How many bank accounts are you hiding, Rich? Hah! Your name matches your vocation, I just realized. C.F.O. and Head Evangelist. You know what happened to all that money.

When Exhibit A came back we had "heart talks". You remember, that was when you wanted to find out who was still "with you" when it came to being with the program you were promulgating (i.e., growing your megachurch). I cancelled a much needed vacation, my first in about four years – my good friend was getting married in California – and I gave that up, and I made my appointment because I thought it was important for my soul. You see, I really did care about my soul. Still do.

"Dog Mom" was my area leader. I went to her new one bedroom on 79th and Broadway. We sat on her bed and she interviewed me. Asked why she'd heard that I was angry and difficult to deal with. I said it was because I wasn't being treated well by the women in charge of our little section of the church, our bible study. They had lied about some things and refused to acknowledge it. We had made agreements and they had broken them.

She had no patience for me. Said that the bible says a church member can't be angry and divisive. (I had, of course, caught them in their lies and confronted them and they ignored me). And that *I* was going to hell. So she was *taking me off the church* roll. *(Astonished.)* She had a list of members in her hand. What flashed in my mind was, "I supported this church for years. I've paid your salary and your endless expenses, and *you're* taking *me* off the roll?" And I watched her as she crossed my name off the list. I was shocked beyond words. She didn't listen to my side of the story. She told me I was going to hell. I didn't believe that for a second. And then she told me I could leave. She was running behind and there was nothing else to talk about. I walked past the others waiting for their heart talks. And I went out into the street and walked back home up Broadway.

I never felt I had done anything wrong. *(Pause.)* Never have. But that moment still hurts, five years later.

(She pauses and shuffles some papers around. She does a double take at something on the paper and makes some calculations for a moment.)

She did me a favor by kicking me out. The best thing that ever happened to me in my life. Thank you, Exhibit A, God's Intolerant Bitch.

(She stacks all her papers neatly in a row. Pause.)

I've been doing a lot of thinking and I've come to this conclusion. The Lord…doesn't trust you, you see. He doesn't like what you've done with his words, his Word. Words mean nothing to you, you use them like weapons. Why don't you just leave people alone? Inserting yourself between someone and her perfectly good life, insisting that she give up everything she loves, everything she ever wanted to be. Her voice, her free will. Inserting your pathetic self between her and her eternal karmic destiny. Why did you do that? I don't understand. I'm not like you. I don't need to destroy things to make myself feel alive. You taught me that. So.

(She gestures to the pile of documents.)

Here's a message from *my* people. My *lawyer*, in fact. I've looked over my current assets, and old records - bank statements, rental contracts, and a list of insured household and big-ticket items.

Let's just split this half and half. You owe me for three years, five months and twelve and a half days of service. Actually, of servitude. It's only $12,341. A bargain. Here is my bill. I'll take it in cash.

(She places the letter in her outbox.)

(She thinks for a moment, then speaks.)

I really hope you get your life together, Rich. There's no need to behave like this. Think of your wife, your daughters. Do you really think they haven't caught on to you already? Don't throw your life away, give up this stupid game. God doesn't love you any less that he does anyone else on this planet. Feel your own soul. Be grateful for your own spark of life. Feed your own soul. You can do it. Go get some bacon. Eggs. Get your own frying pan. Jump on in there, you won't perish. You won't perish if you really feel your own life. Do it. Do it…And get me my settlement by June 1st. I'm going to Tahiti.

(The lights begin to fade. A spotlight hits the letter in the outbox. It gradually dims until the stage is in darkness.)

END OF PLAY.

THE LAST STONE –
OR, THE ADULTERESS SPEAKS FOR HERSELF

Development History

The playwright read THE LAST STONE - OR, THE ADULTERESS SPEAKS FOR HERSELF at the NO PASSPORT/Hibernating Rattlesnakes event on January 25, 2010 at the Nuyorican Poets Café in New York City. She also read MARIA, THE DAY AFTER and “Haiti Calling” that evening.

Character

JUDITH, THE ADULTERESS WHOM JESUS SAVED FROM DEATH

Place

The Courtyard of the Temple in Jerusalem.

Time

The Distant Past.

JUDITH

We were in the midst of something, a lick or kiss, perhaps.

And suddenly the door burst open, it was dark – torches, shouts and condemnation.

He grabbed me by the hair, not my Aaron, but someone – old, shouting, cursing my parents.

I felt blinded, numbed, ripped from my lover's arms and shoved on the ground. Violence – something I was not accustomed to.

I covered my nakedness and found myself stared at – twelve pairs of eyes - and him running. Blinding pain and shock of heart, loss. Loss of heat.

I don't know still what happened, only that I was in the middle of it.

Why did they do this thing – to me and not to my Aaron? They didn't know how I felt about him – the love, the longing, and yes, desire. Desire – a woman feels desire, it keeps her alive. I want more than I have now. I must, to keep alive, you see past the water-fetching and meal-making, I cannot go outside the house and so when I saw that someone looked into my eyes, I gazed back, and fell. I fell into his deep brown eyes. And didn't come back. *(Beat.)* Until now.

There were tears and doubts, fury, longing …damnation. I knew I'd be damned and wanted it anyway. I wanted it, him, to have the closeness. I am a woman first.

The thread kept growing longer, between him and me, to gather us closer when we were apart, it happens that way, you *know*. I wanted him, in every sense of the word, I was honest, I knew what I wanted. I wanted *him*. Not anyone, not money, not everyone, but him. Then. And now. And still.

I do. I do. I say those words for now. Right now, this minute. I do, I do want him now. I shouldn't and I can't but I do. And I will. And I will have him again. No matter what, or how many times they drag me away, or when, or how, or in front of whoever. I am a woman first.

We…need another, for spark, for flame. For sustenance – what does that mean? For a dose of strength. To keep what we have and push it further. Like anyone else. Like everyone else.

"Let him who is without sin cast the first stone."

That's what he said, the Teacher. The one who argues in the Temple. I'd heard about him, and when they threw me at his feet, I feared the worst - the stone. Not the first stone, but the last one - the one that would kill me, rip my artery open, crash against my open brain and deliver the last wound. *(Wistfully)* The last stone – I didn't think of that when I first stared at Aaron with the eyes of my heart and felt the possibility. When my thoughts rushed into the future headlong, gushing like the Spring of Shiloach in late June.

(Beat.)

And now, he's gone, not Aaron, but Jesus. Ripped open with the wound I had feared for myself, heart tearing, arms breaking blood flowing from that sword-rimmed gash. Why – why him and not me? He stepped between me – and the madness.

He came at the right time for me.

And Aaron? He is in my heart and soul, and we have grown apart. We see each other with eyes of comfort, questions, knowing. A long time together brings lovers…love-ers, to a state of grace, which lives outside of time and even gravity. It is an alpha state, unbreachable, eternal. As love burns, it sears a wound, and cauterizes it at the same time.

The last stone. *(She looks straight into the faces of the audience members.)* We all have a last stone. (*Beat.*) Mine doesn't seem so frightening anymore.

(Lights fade.)

END OF PLAY.

Poetry

quartet for change

1

A brown boy was born in Indiana.

His parents were dark-skinned.

He sang and danced and wrote songs.

He grew up to be photographed.

He graced the covers of countless magazines.

Everybody loved him.

As he grew older, his skin changed. It lightened.

Year by year his features became straighter, more angular.

He sang to all of us.

He was the first to sing to help feed Africa.

He had two children.

Then another.

He loved his children.

They loved their daddy.

Only after his death have we seen

That their faces are white.

He, too, died with a white face.

With white children.

And love for all people.

He showed us that God is in us.

Not in our faces.

Not in the shape of our noses.

But underneath our skin.

Michael wore his heart on his sleeve.

But the heart cannot exist outside of the protection of the ribs.

An organ needs bone to sheathe it.

His organs needed sheathing.

He now lives in a casket of bone.

2

A brown boy was born in Hawaii.

His father was dark, his mother was pale.

He grew up and worked very hard.

He was an athlete and a lawyer.

He graced the covers of countless magazines.

He grew up to be President.

He had two brown daughters.

He loved his children.

They love their daddy.

They, too, grace the covers of magazines.

3

Barack loves justice.

He seeks to do well for all men and women.

Michael rode before Barack.

The first took the brunt force of the world.

He made Barack's ride a little bit easier.

4

A life of faith is a gift forever.

Music changes politics.

Art changes the world.

We are the world.

May Paris, Melia and Sasha realize all their dreams.

Notes

The playwright discussed writing ANOTHER WHITE SHIRT on the "Healing the Grieving Heart" internet radio program. Drs. Gloria and Heidi Horsley interviewed her on the topic of "Healing Through the Arts" on a live program on June 3, 2009. The segment is available as a podcast on the Open to Hope website (www.opentohope.com).

WMNF of Tampa, Florida featured the playwright in an interview on the topic of "Healing Through the Arts" on September 4, 2009. She spoke about writing ANOTHER WHITE SHIRT and gave a series of exercises to help others to jumpstart the process of healing through the arts. The radio internet segment aired on the program, "Art in Your Ear" with guest host Dewey Davis-Thompson. You may request a copy of the podcast from the author at hamiltonlit@hotmail.com.

Author's Bio

Anne Hamilton has twenty years of experience in the professional theatre in New York City, across the nation, and abroad. She is the Founder of Hamilton Dramaturgy, an international consulting practice, and has worked with Lynn Nottage, Andrei Serban, The Joseph Papp Public Theater, The Harold Prince Musical Theatre Institute/The Directors Company, Michael Mayer, BT McNicholl, Tina Andrews, Classic Stage Company, George Marcy and Bob Goldstone, Judd Ne'eman, Jean Cocteau Repertory Theater, The Women's Project & Productions, Leslie Lee, Deborah Gregory, The New York City Public Library's Schomberg Center for Research in Black Culture, Andrew Barrett, Warren Bodow, Carrie Robbins, and The University of Iowa Playwrights' Workshop.

Hamilton served as production dramaturg for Classic Stage Company's 1994 NYC premiere of Marivaux's THE TRIUMPH OF LOVE, directed by Michael Mayer.

Leading American actress Kathleen Chalfant starred in her one-woman play AND THEN I WENT INSIDE at the Cherry Lane Theatre in New York City on November 9, 2009. Hamilton then expanded the show into a full-length piece called THE STACY PLAY – A LOVE SONG – VOLUME I, which won a place in TRANSITIONS, a juried Virtual Event at Pen and Brush, the prestigious NYC women's arts collective.

THE STACY PLAY also placed within the top 100 entries of the 79th Annual Writers Digest magazine Stage Play competition (2010).

STAGE DIRECTIONS magazine featured her career in an article on American dramaturgy in April, 2008, naming her an American "trailblazer".

Within the past few years, Hamilton's clients have won significant distinctions in American theatre and film, including: The Pulitzer Prize for Drama, The Tony ® Award; A MacArthur Foundation Fellow Award (the "Genius Award"); first listing in Chuck Davis' "Best Black Plays" volume (best African-American plays of the new century); a semi-finalist standing at the Playwrights Conference at the Eugene O'Neill Theater Center; Best Short Film in the Garden State Film Festival (first film venture); and the selection of a short film created in just three months for screening at the NY AIDS Film Festival in NYC on World AIDS Day, December 1, 2007.

The Bogliasco Foundation of New York City and Bogliasco, Italy awarded her a fellowship in recognition of her personal contribution to the American theatre. She studied the philosophy of aesthetics at St. Catherine's College in Oxford, England, and was a NYSCA auditor for several years. Hamilton holds a Master of Fine Arts degree in Theatre Criticism and Dramaturgy from Columbia University School of the Arts, and also holds dual citizenship in the United States and Italy.

She produces and hosts TheatreNow!, an oral history podcast series of important female American theatre artists, available at http://theatrenow.wordpress.com. She also produces Script Forward!, a specialty e-newsletter for professional scriptwriters.

She has taught dramaturgy at Muhlenberg College, and served as an Adjunct Professor of Theatre at Lehigh University (theatre history).

Hamilton is the past Co-Secretary of the League of Professional Theatre Women, and a member of the Dramatists Guild, LMDA, the UK Dramaturgs' Network and Women in Stage Entertainment (WISE).

She may be reached through hamiltonlit@hotmail.com and www.hamiltonlit.com.

www.ingramcontent.com/pod-product-compliance
Ingram Content Group UK Ltd.
Pitfield, Milton Keynes, MK11 3LW, UK
UKHW041943190726
13854UKWH00004B/1755